18.95

6/15

D1414397

BAND GEEKS
Swing Vote for Solo

Calico

An Imprint of Magic Wagon
www.abdopublishing.com

by Amy Cobb
Illustrated by Anna Cattish

For June and Charlie, an endless source of advice, love, and sweet tea. —AC

www.abdopublishing.com

Published by Magic Wagon, a division of ABDO, PO Box 398166, Minneapolis, Minnesota 55439. Copyright © 2015 by Abdo Consulting Group, Inc. International copyrights reserved in all countries. No part of this book may be reproduced in any form without written permission from the publisher. Calico™ is a trademark and logo of Magic Wagon.

Printed in the United States of America, North Mankato, Minnesota.
102014
012015

Written by Amy Cobb
Illustrations by Anna Cattish
Edited by Rochelle Baltzer & Megan M. Gunderson
Cover and interior design by Candice Keimig

Library of Congress Cataloging-in-Publication Data

Cobb, Amy, author.
  Swing vote for solo / by Amy Cobb ; illustrated by Anna Cattish.
    pages cm. -- (Band geeks)
  Summary: The Benton Bluff Junior High band is one of a number of bands that will compete to perform for a chance to play for the governor, and two of the band members are fighting over who gets to be the soloist--Baylor Meece (clarinet) is not one of them, so can she come up with a plan to bring the band back into harmony?
  ISBN 978-1-62402-078-0
  1. Bands (Music)--Juvenile fiction. 2. Competition (Psychology)--Juvenile fiction. 3. Contests--Juvenile fiction. 4. Middle schools--Juvenile fiction. [1. Bands (Music)--Fiction. 2. Competition (Psychology)--Fiction. 3. Contests--Fiction. 4. Junior high schools--Fiction. 5. Schools--Fiction.] I. Cattish, Anna, illustrator. II. Title.
    PZ7.1.C63Sw 2015
    813.6--dc23
                                          2014029143

With extra special thanks to Larry Vaught for graciously sharing his expertise and passion for music. I am forever grateful to Clelia Gore, Megan Gunderson, and Candice Keimig for taking a chance on me. —AC

TABLE OF CONTENTS

Chapter 1
THE BUZZ

"Let's play that section one more time," Mr. Byrd, our band director, said. He stood on a podium in the middle of the band room. "Pretend the cherry blossoms are in bloom. And really make those bees buzz!"

"Yeah," Yulia Glatt whispered, nudging me with her elbow. "Buzz those bees, Baylor!"

"*Bzz! Bzz!*" I smiled.

We were working on "Flight of the Bumblebee." *Vivace* was typed at the top of our sheet music. That meant we were supposed to play the song lively and quickly. So to make the bees buzz, our fingers had to fly over the keys. Fast!

It was hard to keep up. So our bees didn't exactly sound like they were flitting from cherry blossom

4

to cherry blossom. They sounded more like they were being exterminated. Slowly. And painfully.

But today, Mr. Byrd seemed more determined than ever for us to nail the song. We'd spent almost the entire practice on the same section. "One and two and ready and go!" Mr. Byrd said.

"Wait!" Zac Wiles interrupted. "What measure are we on again?"

"The same one we've been on for the past twenty minutes, Zac." Mr. Byrd took off the straw hat he always wore and fanned himself with it. "Baylor, can you show him please?"

I play the clarinet, and Zac sits behind me, playing the saxophone. "We're right here," I said, turning around to show him.

Zac never takes band seriously. He's always goofing off. But I have to admit, Zac is pretty funny. Most of the time. Just not when he slows us down during practice.

"Keep up, Zac." I whirled back around.

"Keep up, Zac," he imitated me and laughed. "Who are you? Byrd Junior?"

I repositioned my mouthpiece, staring at my music and totally ignoring Zac.

"Okay," Mr. Byrd said. "Play like the musicians you are!" Then he counted for us to begin the section. Again.

When we finished, Mr. Byrd said, "You're making progress. The family Apidae would be proud."

"The family who-dee-what?" Zac asked.

"The family Apidae," Sherman Frye said from the flute section. "That's the scientific name for bumblebees. And other bees, too, like honeybees and cuckoo bees."

"Cuckoo bees? They must've been named after you, Sherman," Zac joked.

"Very funny." Sherman frowned.

"That's enough," Mr. Byrd said. "I have some exciting news to share, so listen up. As some of you may know, the governor's mansion is celebrating

"Okay, guys," Mr. Byrd went on. "I have one other piece of exciting news to share." He wiggled his eyebrows up and down behind his glasses.

What was Mr. Byrd up to now?

"We're going to have a little pre-competition competition right here in the band room," he said. "I've asked a couple of guest judges to help me choose a soloist for our song at the competition."

I didn't like the way this was going. My hands were sweaty just thinking about playing a solo. "Do we have to try out for the solo?" I asked. *Please say no. Because I really, really don't want to.*

"Absolutely!" Mr. Byrd nodded. "It'll be a good experience for everyone. And a fair competition for the solo."

I was afraid he'd say that. But trying out for a solo I didn't even want seemed totally unfair.

"And the song I've chosen for us to play at the competition is one we've practiced a lot lately," Mr. Byrd said. "It's 'Flight of the Bumblebee'!"

By then, the entire band room was buzzing. Everybody talked all at once. They all wanted the solo.

Everyone except me. I felt more like I'd been flying along, minding my own beeswax, until *wham*! I flew face first into one of those giant sticky tape traps dangling from a ceiling. And no matter how much I squirmed to get out of this trap, I was stuck.

Chapter 2

TROUBLE IN THE HIVE

For the next couple of days, the solo audition was big news in the band room. While Mr. Byrd worked with the drummers in the percussion section one day, Lem got the room buzzing again.

"Everyone else may as well give up," Lem said. "You're looking at the soloist. It's *moi.*" He pointed to himself.

Lem's family is from the Philippines. But last year we did a family tree study, and he found out his tree has French roots because, like, a bazillion years ago some relative of his was related by marriage to French royalty. Ever since, Lem has been using French words every chance he gets.

"You're joking, right?" Kori Neal asked.

"Am I laughing?" Lem responded.

"Nope. But you're funny if you think you'll get the solo," Kori said. "I think what this band needs is a trombone solo." She blew into her trombone.

Lem shook his head. "No way! We need a trumpet solo." He blew into his trumpet, pressing a couple of valves up and down quickly.

"Trombone!" Kori said, even louder. This time when she played her trombone, she moved the slide from first to seventh position and back again.

This was turning into a junior high battle of the band instruments. And it had to stop. Now.

"Guys," I said. But they ignored me.

"Everybody loves trumpets more than trombones," Lem went on.

"Who's everybody?" Kori asked. "Not me!"

Then Hope James, my best friend, chimed in. "Hey, who says the solo is going to someone in the brass section, anyway?" She held up her flute. "A woodwind solo would be nice."

"Woodwinds? *Au contraire*," Lem said.

"Maybe I'll get the solo," Zac said from the second row.

Everybody turned around to look at him.

Zac smiled. "I'm just kidding."

"Yeah, that really would be a joke," Lem said.

"*Guys*," I said again. But they still ignored me.

"Whatever," Zac said. "But it's pretty funny how you're all fighting over a dumb band solo." He leaned back in his seat, propped his boots on the back of my chair, and crossed his arms over his camouflage T-shirt. "I mean, who cares?"

"Me!" Lem said. "Do you know how much I practice?"

We all know how much Lem practices. He practices more than anybody else in the band. He practices almost as much as he sleeps, probably.

"Me too! My parents would love for me to win the solo," Hope said.

"I want the solo so Russell can be the star," Kori said. Russell is Kori's trombone.

"Never. Going. To happen," Lem insisted.

"Guys!" I yelled. "Stop!"

They weren't ignoring me now. Everybody was looking at me, including Mr. Byrd.

"Is everything okay over there?" Mr. Byrd asked.

"Yes, sir," I said, lowering my voice.

"Then keep it down, please," Mr. Byrd said, before turning his attention back to Davis Beadle on the snare drum.

While everyone was still quiet, I said, "Zac's sort of right about this."

"You mean, it's funny that we're all fighting?" Kori asked.

"No," I said.

"That we shouldn't care about the solo?" Lem asked.

I shook my head. "No."

"Well, then what is Zac right about?" Hope asked.

"You should care about the solo," I said. "But maybe you shouldn't care so much. All you're doing is fighting. And the judges are the ones who will pick the soloist anyway. Not us."

"That's true," Hope agreed. "I'm sorry."

"Yeah, me too," Kori said.

We all looked at Lem, waiting for him to apologize, too.

"*Touché,*" he finally said, which was probably the closest he'd come to apologizing.

"So how come you're not fighting over the solo like everybody else, Baylor? Don't you want it, too?" Zac asked, nudging my chair with his boot.

"Um, no," I said, turning around in my seat to face him. "I don't want it."

Playing with the entire band was fine. But playing in front of people by myself made me nervous. Super nervous.

Last year at our spring concert, I had to play a section solo. It was just me and two other clarinets. When I looked up and everyone's eyes were on us, I froze. Seriously, I couldn't play a note. So then I did something nobody knows about to this day. Not even Hope. No way did I want another solo.

"How come you don't want it, Zac?" I asked.

"I'd rather be fishing than practicing," he said.

Zac hasn't kept it a secret that his parents signed him up for band, not him. He never does more than he has to. He even spends most of his time trying to get out of that.

"It's a good thing neither of you want it anyway," Lem said. "I mean, don't get your hopes up."

"Yeah, because I'm going to get it," Kori said.

"Nope, it'll be a woodwind," Hope said. "Wait and see."

Great. There they went again. Even though I didn't want the solo, I definitely wanted our band to win a chance to play at the governor's mansion.

But how could we play together as an ensemble when the band was falling apart? Nobody could even get along. That had to change. The competition was coming soon. If Zac could quit goofing off long enough, maybe he could help me.

I turned to face Zac again. "Any ideas about how to make them stop fighting?"

Zac thought for a minute. "I say we have a party."

"A party?" I asked. That wasn't going to work. I should've known Zac wouldn't be any help. I'd have to come up with something on my own. I just wasn't sure what it would be yet.

Chapter 3

A SWEET IDEA

All night, I thought about how to make the band get along again. I had no good ideas. Maybe Zac's party plan wasn't so bad after all.

Really, the more I thought about it, a party might be just what everyone needed. But since hardly anybody was even speaking to anyone else right now, that only left two people to plan the party. Me. And Zac.

"Hey, Zac," I said at the end of band practice that day. "Can I talk to you for a sec? Over there?" I pointed to the lighted trophy case along one wall.

"In private, huh? If you're going to ask me to go to the movies with you, the answer's yes," he joked.

"Sure, we'll go to the movies together. As soon as you can drive over to pick me up," I joked back.

Zac pretended to turn a steering wheel. "Can you wait four years? By then I'll have my license."

"Ha! It'll be hard to wait," I said, "but I'll try."

Even though Zac was joking, I couldn't keep from fast-forwarding ahead four years from seventh grade to our junior year of high school. If he asked me out on a real date then, I wondered if I really would say yes. I mean, Zac is cute. He has these sparkly blue eyes. He does goof off a lot, but he has tons of friends. Everybody likes him, including me.

"So what's up?" Zac asked, leaning against the trophy case.

"Well," I began, "yesterday you suggested we have a party to get everybody to stop fighting."

Zac nodded. "Yeah. And you looked at me like I was crazy."

"Sorry," I said. "It didn't seem like a great idea at first. But this solo thing is totally out of hand."

"Lemme guess. Now that you've thought about it, you think I'm a genius, right?"

I smiled. "If I say yes, will you help me plan the party?"

"Me? How did I get stuck on the party planning committee?" Zac asked.

"Because you and I are basically the only two band members left who are still speaking," I said. "Listen to how quiet the band room is."

Usually at the end of practice, everyone chats and laughs as they take apart their instruments and wait for the bell. But not today. And not yesterday either. Ever since Mr. Byrd announced the solo, the band room had been quiet when instruments weren't being played. Too quiet.

"We're still speaking because neither one of us wants the solo," Zac said.

"Exactly," I agreed.

"And because you think I'm adorable," Zac teased me again.

"Oh, I think you're something," I said.

Zac laughed.

"If we're going to get the band back on track, I need your help," I said. "Are you in?"

"At least you admit you need my help," he said.

"Zac, please be serious."

"Okay, I'll try," he said.

"Can you please try really hard?" There was no way I could make this party happen on my own.

"You're acting like this party is really important."

"It is," I said. "Everybody has to be friends again before we compete, or we'll never earn a spot at the governor's mansion. So the whole band needs us to make this work."

"Fine."

"You mean you'll help?" I asked.

Zac nodded. "What do I have to do?"

"Thank you, Zac!" I pulled out a notebook before he could change his mind. "First, we should decide where we're going to have the party."

"That's easy," Zac said. "The gym. That's where we have all of our school parties."

"Yeah, but then everyone will just shoot hoops or sit on the bleachers all night."

"See? The gym is perfect!"

"No." I shook my head. "If we have it in the gym, that still won't get everyone talking again." I drummed my pencil eraser on my notebook. "Maybe we could rent a place. Someplace small, where everyone has to talk, you know?"

"But where? And how would we pay for it? Byrd won't fork over any cash. He dresses like he's at the beach all the time because he's too tight to pay for a real vacation."

Mr. Byrd was standing by the door wearing a straw hat with a blue band that matched his ocean blue shirt, which was covered with giant tropical flowers. His tube socks with flip-flops made his feet look like goat hooves I'd seen at a petting zoo. It's amazing kids not in band are so afraid of him.

Anyway, Zac was right. Mr. Byrd was long overdue for a vacation. But he tells us that being on vacation is a state of mind, whatever that means. Still, he shows up every day like he's going to hit the beach instead of direct a junior high band.

The bell rang. "There's only one way to find out if Mr. Byrd'll help us," I said. "C'mon!"

Zac followed me to Mr. Byrd. We told him all about how the band was falling apart and about our party idea.

"I love it," Mr. Byrd said.

"So you'll help us pay for it?" I asked.

"No, not me," Mr. Byrd said.

Zac shot me a "told you so!" look. I frowned.

"I said I wouldn't help pay for it, and I won't. But," Mr. Byrd smiled, "I've noticed the tension in here, and I think a party would help settle some jitters. So we can dip into our fund-raising account."

"Thank you, Mr. Byrd!" I shot Zac a "no, I told *you* so!" look.

"What kind of party do you have in mind?" Mr. Byrd asked.

"Something classy," I said.

"A pizza party!" Zac said at the same time.

"So a classy pizza party, huh?" Mr. Byrd laughed. "Plan on having fifty dollars to spend. Now march, before you're late to your next class."

"A pizza party?" I asked Zac as we left.

"Yeah," he said. "Food makes people happy. And even if they're not happy, they can't fight as much when their mouths are stuffed with cheese."

"Then we'd better order extra cheese," I said. As bad as things were, we were going to need it.

Chapter 4

BUSY BEES

It turned out fifty dollars wouldn't buy much. It was just enough to order from Five Buys Pizza Pies, where pizzas were only five bucks each. And there definitely wasn't any cash left over to rent a classy party room. Luckily, Mr. Byrd agreed to let us have the party in the band room.

I was determined, though, that we'd at least decorate the band room for our party. But that meant making the decorations. All of them. Zac was supposed to come over to my house to help out, but he was late. Since the party was tomorrow, I'd started without him.

I had already traced and cut out about fifty treble clefs and music notes from black construction paper when Zac finally showed up.

"Whoa! It looks like a craft store hurled all over your table," he said.

"Zac, where have you been?" I asked.

"Fishing."

"Did some of the fish swim into your pockets?" I pulled up the collar of my T-shirt to cover my nose. "You smell terrible!"

Zac pulled out breath spray and squirted it on his clothes like it was cologne. "Better?"

I breathed deep and nodded. "A little. At least now you smell like minty-fresh fish."

Zac smiled and sat down. "So what are we doing?"

"All of these music notes I cut out need glitter."

"I can glitterize 'em. Watch this." He squeezed the tube. "The top'll shoot off like a rocket."

"Zac, no!"

But it was too late. The top did shoot off like a rocket. Glitter exploded from the bottle and rained down from a glittery cloud. It would've almost

been pretty, except now there was a huge mess to
vacuum up.

"Zac!" I said. "You just glitterized the carpet."

"Oops." He grinned. "Sorry."

"It's okay," I said. "But I'll take these." I slid all of
the glitter tubes out of his reach.

"You mean, you're banning me from using glitter?" Zac laughed.

"Forever!" I laughed, too. Then I held up a glass jar and wrapped sheet music around it. "Okay, so you can work on our centerpieces. Just cut the sheet music to fit, and tape it on. Then we can put some battery-operated tea lights inside. See?"

"Yeah." Zac nodded. "If I'd known we were cutting up sheet music, I would've brought mine."

"These are just some old piano books my mom bought at a yard sale when she got the idea to take piano lessons but never did. We're recycling," I said. "Besides, I'm not so sure Mr. Byrd would like you cutting up your music."

"Hey, I may as well use it for something." Zac reached for a pair of scissors.

"Here's an idea," I said. "Use it to practice."

"Nah, I'll pass."

I dabbed glue on a treble clef. "If you practiced more, you might think playing sax is fun."

"Doubt it," Zac said.

We sat there for a while working quietly. I glued glitter to construction paper music notes and Zac cut and taped sheet music to jars. Then I had to know something. "Can I ask you a question?"

"You just did. So no." Zac smiled.

"C'mon, Zac!"

"Miss School Newspaper Reporter, are you interviewing me? If so, you'll have to talk to my agent first," he joked.

"No, I'm not writing an article." I shook my head. "I know your parents made you sign up for band, but I wonder if you like it at all?"

"Not really," Zac said.

"How come?" I capped the glitter tube and dusted off my hands on my jeans.

"You ask a lot of questions. My agent's going to charge you a fee for each one." Zac grinned.

"Have your agent send me a bill." I smiled, too.

"I will."

"Seriously," I said. "Don't you like band a teensy, tiny bit?"

Zac finished decorating the jars and started cutting random shapes from the sheet music. After a few minutes, he said, "Do you remember in first grade, how it took me forever to learn to read because the letters got all mixed up?"

"Yeah." For a long time, Zac went to a special reading class.

"That doesn't happen much anymore. But sometimes it does with the music notes. And I don't like it." He put the scissors down. "So I don't even want to try."

I didn't say anything. But I could understand. If that happened to me, it would probably be tough to practice my clarinet, too.

"Besides," Zac went on, "I just like being outside, hanging out in the woods, and slaying fish." He pretended he was reeling one in. "It's the big one. Can he hang it? Yes! Zac Wiles just set a new world record for the biggest fish ever caught!" He pretended to struggle with a really heavy fish.

"Let me get a picture!"

Zac posed, and I pretended to snap a shot.

"Hey, I just thought of something," I said. "Have you tried practicing outside? You could give the squirrels and rabbits a free concert."

"My agent says no free concerts allowed. So the squirrels would have to pay me in nuts, and the rabbits in carrots." He laughed at his joke.

"I'm serious," I said. "About practicing outside, I mean. It might help clear your head."

"I dunno." Zac stuck a spool of black ribbon on his finger and spun it round and round. "So is arts and crafts hour over?"

"I think so," I said. "But I like the shapes you cut from the sheet music. I'll put holes in them and string this ribbon through. It'll look cool hanging on the wall at our party." I grabbed the ribbon from him. "And don't forget, it starts at six o'clock tomorrow night. Since we don't have much money for food, I'm making cookies. Can you still bring sandwiches?"

"Tuna fish, right?" Zac asked.

"Right. And make a new playlist so we have some good songs to listen to."

He gave me a thumbs-up.

"Don't be late," I said.

Before Zac headed out the door, he said, "You can count on me. See you Saturday!"

I hoped I could. Without his help, this party would bomb.

Chapter 5

BUZZZZ OFF!

Zac left before we even got started planning games. So I got up extra early the next morning and searched online for easy group activities.

After that, my dad helped me bake cookies. Dozens of cookies—chocolate chip, oatmeal, and peanut butter. And sugar cookies shaped like music notes. They even had black icing on top.

Mr. Byrd gave Zac and me permission to come to the band room early to decorate before everyone else showed up. But when Dad dropped me off, Mr. Byrd was there but Zac wasn't. He was late. Again.

"Baylor, I see plates and napkins in here, but no cups." Mr. Byrd was looking through a box of supplies he'd carried in for me.

"Drinks!" I smacked my forehead. "I forgot drinks."

"That's okay," Mr. Byrd said. Then he pulled open his top desk drawer. It was stuffed with ketchup packets, straws, and napkins. He pushed aside some salt and pepper packets. In the very back were packets of Kool-Aid. He held them up. "Fruit punch and lemonade."

"Wow!" I said. "You have everything in there."

"I've directed junior high band long enough that I'm prepared for almost anything." Mr. Byrd smiled. "There are some pitchers and sugar in the teacher's lounge, so I'll run down and mix this up. I'm sure I can scrounge up some cups there, too."

"Thank you, Mr. Byrd!"

While he was gone, I decorated the band room by myself. The treble clefs and music notes glittered from the ceiling and the walls. The sheet music centerpieces Zac had made lit up tables around the room with their battery-operated tea lights.

I'd punched holes in the shapes Zac had cut from sheet music and run ribbon through them to make a banner. I'd just taped them up when Zac breezed in carrying a cooler.

"Here are the sandwiches." Zac flipped up the lid to show me. "So what's up, Baylor?"

"The decorations," I mumbled. *No thanks to you*, I thought.

"They look nice." Zac gave me a thumbs-up.

If that was supposed to make up for him not showing up to help out, it didn't work. Zac had said I could count on him. But really, I couldn't. He'd proved that again.

"I have a surprise," Zac went on.

"The real surprise would've been if you'd, you know, showed up to help me."

Zac didn't say anything at first. Probably because he knew that other than helping for an hour yesterday, he'd been practically zero help. And he had suggested the party to begin with!

"I'm sorry," he finally said.

"No, I'm sorry, Zac. Maybe I shouldn't have asked you to help me in the first place."

It was probably my fault. I knew Zac was a goof-off, and I asked for his help anyway. But only because the solo audition for the competition had the entire band arguing. Everyone except Zac and me. Until now.

"But," Zac began, "I want to show you—"

"Baylor!" Hope interrupted as she came in. "It looks amazing in here!"

"Thanks," I said.

"Did you do this yourself?" Hope asked.

I looked at Zac. "Mostly." Then I looked at Hope. "Could you help me finish setting up games?"

"Sure!" Hope linked her arm through mine. "Let's go."

I noticed Zac left the band room after that. But I didn't have time to think about him anymore because Hope and I were busy setting up games.

By the time we were finished, Mr. Byrd was back from the teacher's lounge with punch, lemonade, and cups. And almost everyone else had arrived. Zac was back, too. Wherever he had gone, he wasn't gone long.

"Thanks for coming, everyone," I said. "We're still waiting for the pizza delivery, so we'll start off with games." Since most of the band wasn't exactly on speaking terms these days, I had chosen games where everyone had to talk and work together.

While I grabbed the box of game supplies, Mr. Byrd said a few words. "Before we have some fun, let's give Baylor a round of applause for putting this party together for all of us."

Everyone clapped. A few people even whistled.

"Thanks, guys," I said. "But we should also thank Mr. Byrd for letting us use the fund-raiser money and the band room."

Mr. Byrd smiled when everyone clapped for him, too. "My pleasure," he said.

"And," I continued, "I can't take all of the credit. Zac helped, too."

Lem whistled and said, "Way to go, Zac!"

Zac readjusted his camouflage cap lower over his eyes, like he was embarrassed. "I didn't do much," he said.

At least he was honest.

"Okay. Mr. Byrd, you're going to love our first game." I held up a brown paper bag filled with strips of paper. "It's called Composer Match-Up. I'm going to tape either a composer's first or last name to the back of your shirt. Then you have to go around the room until you find your match. That will be the person who has the other half of the composer's name."

"Like someone will have Antonio and someone else will have Vivaldi?" Hope asked.

"Exactly," I said.

Mr. Byrd clapped. "Learning and fun! I do love this game, Baylor."

I smiled. "Line up, everyone."

When I got to Hope, she said, "I'll tape a name on your back, so you can play, too."

"Thanks!" I said, turning around.

After everyone came through the line, I said, "Okay, go find your composer match! If you don't know the composer, just ask someone for help!"

I cheated just a little. Since Lem and Kori were arguing the most, I made sure they were a match. I gave Kori the first name Johannes. Lem got the last name Brahms.

Apparently I wasn't the only one with that idea. I thought Zac wasn't playing because he never came through my line. But somehow, he was my composer match. I had Gershwin, one of my favorites. He had George.

It had to be Hope who had matched us up. Sneaky! If she wasn't my best friend, she would so get it.

She smiled at me then. And I knew I was right.

But Hope wasn't the only one smiling. Everybody else was, too. And talking. The party was actually working. There was peace in the band again. Finally!

Well, mostly peace. Zac stood next to me, but I still didn't feel like talking to him much right now. Not after he'd ditched me.

But I could worry about Zac later. While everyone was getting along, I started another

game. "Next we're going to divide into teams and play Shoe Scramble."

"Shoe Scramble?" Kori asked.

"Yeah." I nodded. "Everyone will take off their shoes, put them in a pile, and mix them all up. Then we'll divide into teams. The first team to find all their shoes and get them back on wins."

Everybody started tossing shoes. In no time, we made a mountain of sneakers and flats, some stinkier than others. Then we formed two teams, both ready to dive in.

"Wait, who's going to be the judge?" Lem asked.

"Mr. Byrd, can you?" I said.

"Of course," he said, swallowing his lemonade. "Get ready. Get set. Go!"

It was chaos. Everybody was pushing and shoving and digging through the pile to find the right shoes. But they were laughing and having fun.

Mr. Byrd declared the team I was on the winner just as Sherman walked in carrying two big trash bags.

"Greetings, fellow band party animals!" he said. "Sorry I'm late, but look what I have." Sherman dumped out tons of balloons. They scattered all across the floor.

"Sherman!" I said. "These balloons are awesome! Thanks for bringing them. What's a party without them?"

"Yeah," he said. "But I didn't bring them."

"You didn't?" I asked.

"No, I found them outside the back entrance by the dumpster. I thought it was just trash someone left lying around, but one of the balloons had fallen out on the ground. Then I saw both bags were full of them."

"You found all of these balloons?" I asked. "Why would anyone blow them up and then just leave them like that?"

"Beats me." Sherman shrugged.

"This sounds like a mystery," I said.

"Uh-oh!" Hope smiled. "Fuzzy Waffles is on the case again."

"And I won't stop until I find out who done it!" I laughed. Fuzzy Waffles is my top secret detective name, even though it isn't really much of a secret. Everybody knows I love spy movies. And I'm always looking for a mystery to solve. "Did you see anybody around the dumpster, Sherman?"

He shook his head. "Nope. Nobody."

"This mystery might be a tough case without any clues. But maybe there are some fingerprints." I inspected a balloon.

Hope batted the balloon out of my hands. "C'mon, Baylor. It's a party. Save your detective work for later."

"Balloons are dumb anyway," Zac said. "Who wants to hear some music?"

"Me!" Sherman said. "Prepare to be jealous of my moves." He started twirling all around, his curly brown hair bouncing up and down, before Zac even played the first song.

While we listened to music, everybody tossed around the balloons and had balloon fights. We even made teams and raced to see who could build the biggest tower by taping balloons together.

By then, it was almost time for the pizzas to arrive, so I said, "We have time for one more game. I'll tape a piece of paper to your back."

"Again?" Lem asked.

"Shh, listen," Kori told him.

"This'll be fun," I said. "The piece of paper will have a name on it. This will be the name of your band instrument. But you have to go around and ask people to give you clues to figure out what that name is."

"My flute doesn't have a name," Sherman said.

"Neither does my clarinet," I said. "We're pretending, just for fun to see what name you'd end up with if you named it. So, like, you might get Jet for your flute's name, Sherman. Or somebody might get Shark."

"I only know one person ever who named her instrument," Lem said, looking at Kori.

Kori shot Lem a look like my cat gives the neighbor's dog. Her claws were out.

"What?" Lem said. "I think it's strange."

"Watch it, Lem," Kori said.

"Well, it is. And Russell?" Lem shook his head. "That's just weird."

Everyone stepped back then because we all know Kori's trombone is named Russell after her dad. He moved out a while back. She said calling her trombone Russell helped her feel closer to him.

"Maybe I think *you're* weird," Kori said.

"*C'est la vie*," Lem said.

Kori put her hands on her hips. "Point proven! Nobody even knows what that means."

"It means 'that's life.' So if you think I'm weird, so what." Lem said. "That's life."

"Never mind," I said. "Let's just forget this game." My plan was to bring peace back to the band, not make them fight even more.

"You're just some French wannabe," Kori said. "You're not really French, so that's life. Real life!"

"You're just jealous because your real life is going to be listening to me play the solo I'll win at the audition next week." Lem crossed his arms.

Just great. Things had been going so well, too. Almost too well. And now Kori and Lem were arguing about the solo again. In a way, things were worse than ever.

At least before, Zac and I were working together. But now we weren't exactly getting along either. I mean, it's not like I wanted to be mad at Zac. But he showed up late both times I needed his help. He just didn't seem to care about band the way I did. I'd never ask Zac to help with anything else. Ever.

It was up to me to fix this by myself. And the way Kori and Lem were arguing, I had to think of something fast.

But what? I was all out of ideas.

Chapter 6
A NEW BEE-GINNING

That's when I spotted the pizza delivery guy coming up to the door.

"Five Buys Pizza Pies delivery," a skinny teenager said when I let him in. He was practically hidden behind his tower of pizza boxes.

"You're here!" I said. "I'm so glad to see you!" If his arms hadn't been overflowing with pizzas, I might've hugged him. I think I did jump up and down a little.

He raised one eyebrow, probably because he wasn't used to people being this excited to see him. But to me, he wasn't just a pizza delivery guy. Nope. Inside those boxes lay pizza power. Maybe if everyone started eating, they'd stop fighting. Like Zac had said, the band couldn't argue if their mouths were full of pizza.

"Can you put them on this table?" I asked. "And could you hurry, please?"

Now both eyebrows shot up. But he followed me to the table and set up a tower of pizza boxes.

"Enjoy," he said, turning to go after I handed him the fund-raiser cash.

"Thanks! We will!" Then I cupped my hands around my mouth so everyone could hear me. "Guys, look! The pizzas are here!" I raised the top of one of the boxes. "Sausage. It smells yummy!"

Mr. Byrd grabbed a plate and a slice of pizza and took a bite. "This is great, Baylor," he said. It must've been. Cheese strung from his lips to his plate. But nobody else came to get in line.

Then Kori yelled at Lem. "You don't have a chance!"

"Mr. Byrd, aren't you going to make them stop?" I asked.

He dabbed at his chin with a napkin. "I could do that," he said. "And it would solve things momentarily. But I've found as long as it doesn't go too far, it's best to let students work things out on their own."

I hate it when grown-ups do that. The band was being ripped apart, like the sausage ball on Mr. Byrd's pizza. If he wasn't going to stop it, I would. Or at least, I'd try.

I opened two more boxes. "And look! Here's cheese and pepperoni!"

Still nobody came over to grab a plate.

They probably didn't even notice me because Kori and Lem kept arguing.

Lem said, "No, you don't have a chance with your school-loaner trombone!"

"Shut it, Lem!" Kori shot back.

Some of the band members formed a circle around Kori. Others gathered around Lem. They were taking sides. This was getting worse!

"Get a slice while it's hot!" I said, getting even louder.

Zac ran over and started putting pizza on plates.

"What are you doing?" I asked.

He pretended to smooth his imaginary handlebar moustache. "If the band won't come to the pizza pie, then the pizza pie must go to the band," he said in a terrible Italian accent.

I couldn't keep from smiling.

Then Zac started passing out plates. "Pizza!" he called. "Get your pizza!"

Kids actually started taking plates from Zac, as fast as he could pass them out. So I started piling pizza on plates. Zac handed them out, and I had more ready when he came back over to get them.

I poured drinks next, and Zac handed them out, too. Pretty soon, we were all out of pizza. And almost out of lemonade and punch.

"This isn't good," I said to Zac. "All that's left to feed them is my cookies."

"Don't worry." Zac ran over to his cooler and came back carrying a plate. He lifted off the tinfoil.

It was the sandwiches! I'd forgotten about Zac bringing them. "You're a lifesaver!" I smiled.

But the smell was really fishy, even for tuna fish. "Did they go bad?" I asked.

I wanted to stuff my head inside an empty pizza box to escape the smell, but that would be rude. And kind of weird. So I tried holding my breath, instead.

"Nah, they didn't go bad. I packed them in ice."

So just like with the pizzas, we started an assembly line. I put sandwiches on plates, and Zac passed them out. Except by then, everyone must've been full. The sandwiches didn't go as fast.

When Zac couldn't get anyone else to take a sandwich, he came back to where I stood by the food table.

"Thanks for helping me out," I said.

Zac shrugged. "No problem."

He really had helped me out, too. I'd sworn I wasn't going to ask for his help ever again. And I didn't. Zac just sort of came to my rescue. Maybe he cared about band more than I thought he did.

"I'm sorry about earlier," I said. "I was sort of grumpy from getting up early and all of the planning, I guess."

"Me too," Zac said. "Sorry about being late, I mean."

"Friends again?" I held out my hand.

"Since you begged." Zac smiled and shook my hand.

I smiled, too. "Well, no pizza left for these two friends, huh?" I asked.

"That's okay," Zac said. "At least we still have sandwiches." He reached for one and bit into it.

He chewed like it was okay, so I grabbed one, too. But it was a mistake.

I bit into it and chewed. And chewed. The more I chewed, the bigger it got. I couldn't swallow it. But I didn't want to hurt Zac's feelings. So when he wasn't looking, I spit it into my napkin and swished lemonade around in my mouth to replace the fishy taste.

I wondered what went wrong with Zac's recipe. "That wasn't like any tuna fish I've ever tasted before. Did you do something special?"

Being a reporter for the school newspaper had taught me a lot of skills about interviewing people, because before, I probably would've blurted out, "Why is this tuna so disgusting?!"

"It's good, isn't it?" Zac smiled. "But it's not tuna fish."

"It isn't?"

"Nah, we were all out of tuna. Good thing I caught a lot of fish yesterday."

"You mean—"

Zac nodded. "Yep, I mixed up all of the fish I caught, boiled 'em, and whipped 'em up with some mayonnaise and relish. That was blue gill and catfish. I call it a blatfish sandwich." He smiled. "Pretty good, right?"

I nodded. That was another reporter skill. Sometimes, it was best to listen, without saying anything at all. Like now.

Chapter 7

PLAN BEE

Listening! That was it! Since the party hadn't gone exactly as planned, first thing on Monday I talked to Mr. Byrd about my new plan. I knew this one would work. It had to.

"Good morning, Baylor," Mr. Byrd said, unlocking the band room door. "What brings you by so early?"

"I need a favor," I said, following him to his desk.

He hung up his coat next to his Class of '92 band jacket and sat down. "What can I help you with?"

"It's just nobody is getting along right now. And we have this big competition coming up. Our band is good enough to win. I know it. But I'm worried we'll lose because we won't play our best if everyone is arguing." I finally took a breath.

I tried, but I couldn't keep from worrying. Hope always teases me about having a built-in worry meter. And the more I worry, the faster I talk.

Mr. Byrd knew it, too, because he said, "Calm down, Baylor. It's not that bad, is it?"

I nodded. "Yes, sir. It is. Kori and Lem can't stand the sight of each other. I've even heard a couple of kids say they might quit band."

Mr. Byrd cleaned his glasses on his tropical shirt, this one featuring palm trees at sunset. "I suspect this will all blow over after the solo auditions. But in the meantime, what do you suggest?"

I was glad he asked. "Band buddies."

"Go on," Mr. Byrd said.

So I told him all about my idea to have everyone team up. I finished with, "If people work together, they'll help each other. So they'll listen to each other more. And maybe argue less."

"Pairs working together? That's a great idea!" Mr. Byrd said. "I'll let everyone know this afternoon."

"Thank you, sir." I smiled.

"And thank you, Baylor, for caring so much."

"I just want everyone to get along." I turned to go. "Like they used to," I said to myself, closing the band room door behind me.

That afternoon at practice, I was nervous. It was our first time together as a group since our party disaster Saturday night. I wasn't sure how it would go. But basically, everybody put together their instruments and sat in silence until Mr. Byrd said, "First chairs, tune your sections."

"Wait! I didn't know we were playing today," Zac began. "You won't believe it, but I forgot my sax."

Mr. Byrd silently held up a hall pass.

For the next few minutes, the band room sounded like a zoo. A loud zoo, with all of the animals roaring and chirping at the same time. After that came scales, followed by more tuning.

Then we played some easier songs from our band book before Mr. Byrd said, "Please take out 'Flight of the Bumblebee.'"

Mr. Byrd counted off, "One and two and . . ."

We only played four measures before Mr. Byrd stopped us. "I want you to play that again. Do it just like that, except this time, attack the notes. Smooth out those runs so we're more in time."

Mr. Byrd led us through the same measures at least ten times before we finally moved on. By then, my bumblebee was getting tired, but I knew Mr. Byrd only wanted us to play our best.

That's how we finished up practice, repeating different measures over and over again. We worked on timing and articulation and a bunch of other itty-bitty things. But when we put them all together, we were actually starting to sound pretty good.

"Now that Zac is back," Mr. Byrd said before the bell rang, "I have special news to share with you."

I heard Kori mumble, "What now?"

And Lem said, "He's probably going to cancel solo auditions. The clear choice is *moi.*"

"Have you heard of the buddy system when it comes to swimming?" Mr. Byrd continued. "You never head to the pool alone. Buddies look out for each other."

"Are we having a pool party?" Zac asked.

"Cowabunga!" Sherman said, catching a pretend wave.

"Sort of." Mr. Byrd smiled. "But not exactly."

"Huh?" Sherman said.

"For the rest of this week, you'll be assigned a Band Buddy. You'll spend part of each class working closely with this person on 'Flight of the Bumblebee' to make sure everyone is ready for our governor's mansion competition."

"Can I be my own buddy?" Zac asked.

"No, you may not," Mr. Byrd said. "And each day, you'll have a new buddy."

Oh, Mr. Byrd was good! I hadn't even thought about switching up partners like that.

"I have Band Buddy schedules typed up. Grab one before you go," Mr. Byrd said.

When everyone was in the hall heading to our next class, I heard Kori mumble, "Just great. I'm stuck with Lem on Friday."

"No, I'm stuck with you," Lem shot back.

And listening to them argue right now, I felt double stuck. With both of them.

Chapter 8
BUDS IN BLOOM

"Baylor!" Hope hugged me the next day at practice. "We're Band Buddies!"

"This is going to be so awesome!" I said.

And it was. We made a super team.

We even had time to plan our sleepover at Hope's house on Saturday night after solo auditions. And to talk about the mysterious band party balloons.

"I didn't forget about them, you know," I said.

Hope smiled. "I knew you wouldn't give up on the case, Fuzzy Waffles. Do you have any clues?"

"Maybe." I smiled.

The next day, Kori was my Band Buddy. It wasn't so awesome.

"This is dumb," Kori said.

I shook my head. "It's not dumb. It'll be fun."

I stood up and headed toward Mr. Byrd.

"Hey, where are you going?"

I smiled. "You'll see!"

A few minutes later, I sat down beside Zac again. "Here, *you* play like the musician you are," I said, shoving some sheet music at him.

"What am I supposed to do with this?"

"Put it on your stand."

He did. Upside down.

"Zac!"

He laughed. But I didn't think it was funny. I knew Zac would be great if he'd just be serious.

Kori wasn't laughing either. "I can't work with you anymore!" she yelled at Lem.

"I can't help it if I show you up!" Lem shot back.

Kori waved her finger in front of Lem's face. "You ain't showin' me up!"

"*Au contraire!*" Lem said, holding up his trumpet like a trophy. "And tomorrow, I'm going to show you up again when I win the solo."

"Don't bet on it! That solo is mine!" Kori said.

Zac looked at me. "They just snapped."

"Yeah," I said. "I don't care who gets the solo tomorrow. I just want this to be over with."

"Maybe you'll get it," Zac said.

"No way!" I said. "I don't want it."

Okay, correction. I didn't care who got the solo, as long as it wasn't me. And I had no worries about that happening.

Chapter 9

QUEEN BEE

"I'm super nervous," Hope said, sliding down the bleacher to sit beside me. She fidgeted with the belt on her dress. "You're so lucky your mom didn't make you dress up."

It was Saturday, and the entire band was gathered in the gym for solo auditions. Everyone had to play for Mr. Byrd and two other judges. And he'd said one of the judges would be a big surprise.

I agreed with Hope. I'm lucky my mom is a lot more laid-back than hers when it comes to band. This morning, she'd told me to wear something nice, but comfortable. So I wore my purple sweater, my favorite pants, and my new boots.

Hope nodded. "Mom said I should dress like I've already won the solo in order to win it for real."

"I bet you will," I said. Then I smiled. "You probably would win even if you wore a bathrobe."

Hope smiled, too. "Thanks! But what do you think about Kori's chances? Wasn't she one of your Band Buddies?"

"Yep. And she's really good, too."

"So is Lem," Hope said. "He was my Band Buddy on Thursday. He wants it so bad."

"They both do. Too bad it couldn't be a duet." I laughed. "Can't you see Lem and Kori playing a duet at the governor's mansion?"

Hope laughed, too. "They'd probably end up fighting right there in front of Governor Shaffer."

"Yeah," I said. "Kori would probably bump Lem with her trombone slide. And then Lem would empty his spit valve on Kori's shoes."

"Eww!" Hope made a face. "And when the governor came over to split them up, he'd slip on the wet floor and end up wiping out the entire brass section."

"Now that would be front-page news. 'Benton Bluff Junior High Band Banned from Governor's Mansion Forever'!"

"You write the article, and I'll snap the pictures." Hope is a *Bloodhound* photographer.

"Deal!" I said, and we both laughed again.

Zac came strutting over then and sat behind us. "What's so funny?"

"Nothing," Hope said.

"It must've been something," Zac said.

Best friends sometimes think things are funny that no one else gets. I knew Zac wouldn't think the newspaper headline was as funny as Hope and I did, so I just said, "We were laughing about duets."

"Seriously? Since when have duets been so hilarious?" Zac asked.

Hope and I looked at each other and burst out laughing again.

"Since Kori hit Lem. And Lem emptied his spit valve on Kori. And the governor . . . ," Hope said.

"And the governor wiped out the whole brass section and banned us from the mansion," I added.

Zac shook his head. "You two are cra-zy."

Hope looked at me. "He said we're crazy!" Then she doubled over laughing.

"See what I mean?" Zac circled his finger around his ear.

"I think Hope's nervous-laughing now," I said.

Hope could talk about me being a motormouth all she wanted. We've been best friends since we were five. But let me tell you, Hope James is a nervous laugher. I knew it the first time we sneaked off of our kindergarten nap mats. Mrs. Gaines busted us in thirty seconds because Hope would not. Quit. Laughing.

"Hope," I leaned over and said, "pull yourself together."

She dabbed at the tears in her eyes with the back of her hand. When Hope laughs that hard, she always cries. She took a couple of deep breaths.

"That's it," I said. "Calm down."

She did. And just in time, too. Because Mr. Byrd was standing at the gym door.

"Hope James," he said.

Hope grabbed her flute and sheet music and made her way down the bleachers.

"Good luck, Hope!" I called after her.

"She doesn't need luck," Zac said, sliding down into Hope's spot beside me.

Zac was right. After Lem, Hope probably practiced more than anybody else we knew.

"How about you?" I smiled. "Do you need luck?"

"Nah, the judges need luck, not me. They'll be lucky if my playing doesn't make their ears bleed." Zac grinned.

"Maybe you'll surprise them. And surprise yourself," I said.

"Uh-huh." Zac laughed. "You really are crazy."

"Hey, speaking of surprises, what surprise were you talking about at the band party last weekend?"

Zac didn't say anything. He looked down at his boots, suddenly really interested in scraping a clump of dried dirt from one toe.

"You said you had a surprise to show me," I went on. "Right before Hope came in."

Zac scraped even harder at the dirt. He ground it into a fine brown powder between his feet.

"Zac?" I waved my hand in front of him.

"It doesn't matter now," he finally said.

But it mattered to me. I wished I knew what it was. "C'mon, Zac." I nudged his shoulder.

"Hey, I'm not talkin' without my lawyer present," he joked.

"You mean your agent?"

"No, silly," he said. "I mean my lawyer. I have both."

"You're the one who's crazy, Zac Wiles."

By then, the gym door was opening again. And Mr. Byrd stood there, calling my name this time. "Baylor Meece! You're up."

I froze for a second.

"Baylor, that's you." Zac elbowed me.

For the first time since Mr. Byrd announced there would be a solo part, I was nervous. Mega nervous! I reached for my clarinet case. And I don't remember much after that.

Somehow, I ended up front and center in the band room with my clarinet. Mr. Byrd and Mrs. Schwartz, the high school band director, sat at a table facing me.

"Our special guest judge took a break and should return any minute," Mr. Byrd said.

"I'm sorry to keep you waiting," came an unfamiliar voice.

When I looked up from arranging my sheet music on the stand, I couldn't believe it. "You're Rube Chenault!" I said.

Rube Chenault is a well-known local jazz musician. And he looked just like he does in pictures. His hair was silvery-black, and he wore a pinstripe purple vest buttoned over an olive green shirt. He even wore his famous shiny gold bow tie.

"And let's see here," he said, sitting down beside Mr. Byrd and glancing at a sheet of paper on the clipboard in front of him. "You're Baylor Meece." He looked up at me. "I'm happy to make your acquaintance, Baylor. Call me Rube."

Oh. My. Gosh. Rube Chenault knew my name! Well, sort of. He had to read the audition sheet. But still! He knew that I existed in the world and that was insane.

"I can't believe it!" I said. "My grandpa has, like, every one of your CDs."

"Your grandpa?" Rube asked. "Don't you have any of my music?"

"Um, no. But I've listened to Grandpa's a lot."

Rube smiled. "This old man is only teasing you."

"Oh." I smiled too. "But I really have listened to your songs a lot. When you play trumpet, it's . . . I can't even keep my feet still. They just tap along."

"Whoo-wee!" Rube slapped his knee. "I like this child already. But she's gonna make my head swell up till I can't even squeeze it through the band room door."

"Don't you worry, Rube. We won't let you get stuck in here," Mr. Byrd said.

"I'm counting on you now." Rube laughed. His laugh bounced off the walls. It was deep and rich, just like the jazz music he played.

Mr. Byrd looked at me then. "Ready, Baylor?"

"Yes, sir," I said.

"Then please, take it away," Mr. Byrd said.

I licked my lips and put them over my mouthpiece. For a second, my mind flashed back to last year's spring concert. Except this time, I didn't have anyone playing beside me. I was on my own. So what I did then wouldn't work now.

But I had a chance to play in front of Rube Chenault. *The* Rube Chenault. And he said he liked me. Plus, I really liked the fast tempo of "Flight of the

Bumblebee." It was fun to play. And that's exactly what I decided to do—just have fun playing it.

So I blew into my clarinet, and my bumblebees took flight. They soared over my head and up to the rafters and filled up the entire room. Those bees buzzed like never before.

When I finished playing, Mr. Byrd, Rube, and Mrs. Schwartz all clapped.

"Well done," Mr. Byrd said.

Rube nodded. "Yes, indeed."

Mrs. Schwartz smiled as she jotted down some notes.

"Baylor, we're close to wrapping up auditions. Once we've reached a decision, we'll come to the gym to announce our new soloist," Mr. Byrd said.

"Okay, thanks," I said, packing my clarinet back into its blue velvet-lined case. Soon we'd know who the soloist would be—Kori or Lem. Or Hope. She had a good shot, too.

We didn't have to wait long.

Mr. Byrd and Rube came into the gym a few minutes later. Mr. Byrd clapped his hands to get everyone's attention. "Our other judge, Mrs. Schwartz, has left," he said, "but let's thank Mr. Chenault for being here today!"

Everyone cheered and clapped.

Rube looked sort of embarrassed. "Now, you know that's not necessary. It was my pleasure to spend the day with such fine musicians."

Mr. Byrd patted Rube on the back. "Let's move on to announcing the winner of the solo part for the governor's mansion competition. It wasn't an easy decision, was it, sir?" Mr. Byrd looked at Rube.

"No sirree," Rube said. "You're not kidding."

Mr. Byrd handed Rube a piece of paper. "Would you be so kind as to make the announcement?"

"I'd be honored." Rube smiled. "But let me tell all of you fine boys and girls something first." He shook his finger at us. "I was simply amazed at the amount of talent in this junior high band.

"Some of you know you have something special." Rube glanced at Lem. "And some of you haven't even realized it yet. But the potential is there." He looked right at Zac.

Mr. Byrd nodded in agreement.

"But one thing's for sure," Rube went on. "Just like caterpillars, one day each one of you will pop out of your cocoon. And when you do, you're going to fly." He pointed at us again. "Listen to this old man. I know what I'm talking about."

We all clapped again.

"Okay, this is what y'all are really interested in, isn't it?" Rube held up the sheet of paper. "The solo position has been awarded to . . ." He took a deep breath.

I glanced at Lem. He sat on the edge of his seat, ready to spring up when his name was called.

"Baylor Meece!" Rube finished.

I must've heard wrong. "Me?"

"Yes, you!" Hope tugged on my arm.

But I didn't want to stand up. I'd look like a real goof if I did, because for sure I'd heard wrong. Rube *had* to have said someone else's name.

But by now Zac was tugging on my other arm. Even if I'd misunderstood, Zac and Hope wouldn't have, too.

Then Rube pointed at me and said it again. "Baylor Meece, get yourself off of those bleachers and come on down here so we can congratulate you properly."

So for the second time in one day, everything was a blur. The next thing I knew, I stood beside Rube. He shook my hand, and Hope snapped a picture of us together for the school paper.

Mr. Byrd and everyone in the band congratulated me. Well, not everyone. Kori and Lem didn't look very happy. Believe me, they weren't the only ones. I wasn't happy that I'd won either. I mean, the audition was fun. But I still didn't want this solo. How could I get out of it?

Chapter 10

WINGING IT

"I can't play the solo part," I told Hope at her sleepover that night while we played air hockey. She'd somehow convinced her parents to let her have the table in her bedroom.

"If you couldn't, you wouldn't have won the solo." Hope smacked the puck.

"I can play the song. I just can't play it by myself."

"You did it today," Hope pointed out. "It's almost like playing at the governor's mansion competition."

I shook my head. She didn't understand. "I only played for three judges today. That wasn't so bad." I sent the puck sailing back toward Hope's goal.

"But there'll probably be more judges at the governor's mansion competition. And I'll have to play in front of the entire band. Big audiences totally freak me out." I wiped my forehead and showed Hope my hand. "See? I'm sweating already."

"It probably won't be that big of a deal, Baylor."

Hope really didn't get it. I had no choice. I had to come clean.

"Remember the spring concert last year when Becca, Millie, and I played a section solo together?" I asked.

"Of course." Hope nodded. "You guys were awesome together."

"No, they were awesome. Not me." I glanced down at the carpet. "I didn't even play my part."

Hope's hockey mallet hovered above the table. "What do you mean?"

"I mean, I faked it. I moved my fingers over the keys to make it look like I was playing. But really, I wasn't. So Becca and Millie were awesome." I took a deep breath. "But I was just a big, fat faker."

"Wow. Just wow." Hope set down her mallet. "But you're seriously an awesome clarinet player. If you weren't, you wouldn't sit in first chair. So," she leaned against the table, "why did you fake it?"

"I don't know." I shrugged. "Maybe because when the whole band plays together, the audience sees all of us. Nobody focuses on just me. So it's different."

"And when you play alone—" Hope began.

"Then I totally freak out. And freeze up." I flopped down on a beanbag chair. "Help."

Hope sat cross-legged beside me. "A section solo is one thing. Faking your *solo* solo is a no go."

"Yep," I sighed.

Both of us were quiet for a few minutes.

"Unless," I said, "I record myself playing my solo. Then I play the recording at the competition. I'll just move my fingers over the keys so everybody thinks it's me."

"I dunno," Hope said.

"I saw something like that in a spy movie once. It could work."

Hope frowned. "It'd have to be perfect, though. Everybody would see if you were off."

"True," I agreed. "Maybe faking a sickness would be easier. Should I go for a virus? Or fake an allergy?"

"An allergy?" Hope asked.

"Yeah, something like, 'Oh no, Mr. Byrd! I just found out dusty, old governors' mansions make my eyes get all watery. So since I can't read my sheet music, I can't play.'"

Hope shook her head.

"How about a broken bone then? Maybe a rib? No, a finger! Besides," I reminded her, "you know how clumsy I am. It could really happen."

"Mr. Byrd might believe it. But not your mom."

Hope was right again.

"Yeah, she'd probably want an X-ray for proof," I said.

After that, we just sat around brainstorming more ideas.

"What if your great-aunt Ella comes to visit?" Hope asked.

"I don't have a great-aunt Ella. But I suppose Mr. Byrd doesn't know that," I said.

"Then there you go."

"Or," I said, "my guppy died in a tragic fish tank vacuuming accident. I'm too sad to play fast songs."

"Your car broke down, and you can't make it," Hope suggested.

"My mom said I'm not allowed to participate in any fun activities until I clean my room."

"Hey, that sounds like my mom, not your mom." Hope smiled.

"Yeah, my mom is the only mom I know who is messier than her own kids. Dad says when Kennet was a baby, Mom lost him in the clutter one day. They couldn't find him until he started crying."

Kennet's my older brother. His hobbies include making my life miserable and looking for new ways to make my life miserable.

"Too bad they found him," I said. "Or you'd be looking at an only child right now."

Hope laughed.

But I couldn't. Not until we came up with an idea that actually worked. I hugged one knee against my chest and rested my chin on it, trying to think of something—anything!—else.

"Why don't you just give your solo a try?" Hope finally asked.

"Huh?"

"You know, instead of working on not playing your solo, try working on playing your solo."

Me? Play a solo? "Yeah, right," I said.

The other ideas were crazy. But Hope's last idea was the craziest one of all. It would never work.

There was only one day left before the governor's mansion competition. And Hope had kicked her plan into overdrive.

"C'mon, Baylor," Hope said. "Let's go to the park."

The park is only a block away from my house. We go there all the time when Hope comes over. Sometimes we practically own that playground. But this time it was packed. That's because most of the band was there.

"What's going on?" I asked.

"Remember when everyone was fighting about who would win the solo part?" Hope asked.

"Yeah," I said. "It was last week."

Zac smiled. "But you wanted to help get the band back together."

"And now you're upset," Lem said.

"So we wanna help you," Kori added.

Hope nodded. "We don't want you to be nervous tomorrow, so we've got some ideas."

The band showed up here to help me? Even Lem and Kori, who both wanted the solo part so badly? The part that I didn't even want.

I didn't realize they cared this much. "Thanks, guys. But," I sighed, "you're wasting your time. This solo thing is just too much. I'm going to blow it."

"Not if you try yoga!" Sherman slanted both arms toward the sky, forming a Y. Besides being in band together, Sherman and I are also neighbors. So I know he does yoga. A lot.

"Even yoga can't help me," I said.

Sherman unrolled his yoga mat. "It can! You'll see, I promise."

After some stretches, Sherman said, "Now let's strike a pose!" Then he taught me the tree pose, the cat pose, and a warrior pose.

When we were finished, he took me back over to the picnic table where Kori sat. "She's all yours," Sherman said.

Kori didn't waste any time. She got right to it. "Sometimes my little brother and sisters fight until one of 'em explodes."

"Whoa," I said. Kori has to take care of her siblings while her mom works. It actually makes me glad I just have to deal with Kennet.

"Yep," Kori went on. "But I do some deep breathing stuff to calm 'em down. I'll show ya."

She took a deep breath in through her nose and held it, before slowly breathing out through her mouth.

"Now you try," Kori said.

So I did.

"Again," Kori instructed.

And when I was finished, she said, "Good. And the best thing about deep breathing is you can do it anywhere, even at the competition tomorrow." She smiled then. "Seriously, it really works."

Lem leaned on the picnic table. "My turn?"

"Yep," Kori said.

"Ever heard of progressive muscle relaxation, Baylor?" Lem asked.

"Uh, no." I shook my head.

"I researched it," he said. "So listen to *moi*, and I'll teach you. First, think of something stinky."

"Got it," I said. That was easy. My nose still hadn't forgiven me for smelling Zac's blatfish sandwiches.

"Scrunch up your nose, hold it, and then relax those muscles," Lem said.

He also had me pretend to squeeze a squishy ball in my hands and to dig my toes in sand.

"Tomorrow, you'll be the *crème de la crème*, Baylor," Lem said.

"The what?"

Lem smiled. "You'll be the best."

"Thanks, Lem." I smiled, too.

"She's mine!" Hope linked her arm through mine and walked me away from the table. "I'm going to help you with visualization. My mom does it all the time. Close your eyes."

I did.

"Now, picture yourself at the governor's mansion competition tomorrow. Are you there?"

I nodded. "Yep."

"You're standing in front of the judges," Hope continued. "Do you see them?"

"Yep," I said again.

"You're playing your solo better than ever. The judges love it. See them smiling?"

I squeezed my eyes tighter. "The picture's sort of blurry."

"New scene, then. Can you imagine Zac?"

"Yeah." I nodded. "Why?"

"Then picture him heading straight toward you because he really is." Then she whispered, "I think Zac likes you."

My eyes flew open. "Hope!"

She laughed.

"Guess who?" Zac covered my eyes.

"I know it's you, Zac." I turned to face him. "I saw you when we got here."

He grinned. "You noticed."

"Told you so," Hope said.

"Told her what?" Zac asked.

"Nothing." Hope smiled sweetly before running off to the swings with Yulia.

"So what's up, Zac?" I asked.

"Just have fun tomorrow. Then you won't be nervous."

"Fun?" I was playing a solo for some judges I didn't even know. For a competition that decided if our band got a chance to play at the governor's mansion. And if we didn't make it, it would be my fault. This was so *not* fun!

"Yeah," Zac said. "Think of something funny."

I tried. "I can't think of anything," I finally said.

"Nothing?" Zac leaned in close.

"Nothing."

He leaned in even closer until his face was only a few inches from mine. I wasn't sure what he was up to. Then he squinted one eye, snarled his lip, and made a ridiculous face.

I started laughing then because for, like, half a second, I thought Zac was going to kiss me or something. Then Zac made another silly face. And another. The more I laughed, the goofier he got.

"Okay, stop," I said, trying to catch my breath. My sides hurt from laughing so hard.

"See?" Zac said. "Good-bye, nerves."

And for the first time in days, I really wasn't nervous. Too bad it didn't last long.

Chapter 11

BAYLOR'S BUMBLE

"C'mon, Baylor," Hope said, knocking on the bathroom stall door.

I had locked myself in as soon as the band had arrived at the performing arts center.

Hope drummed her fingers on the door. "You can't stay in there forever."

"Just until today is over. Okay?" I mumbled.

"No, it's not okay. Everybody's waiting for you."

I didn't say anything.

"You're not the only one who's nervous!"

Shoes clicked across the tile floor then. "Yeah. Me too." That was Kori's voice.

"See, Baylor?" Hope said. "Everyone's nervous. So come out here and we'll be nervous together."

I still didn't say anything, so she added, "Please."

I couldn't believe Hope was nervous. She always seemed calm. And Kori, too? She acted so cool.

I slid the latch and opened the door just enough to peek out. "Are you kidding?"

"Nope," Kori said. She did look paler than usual.

"We're serious, Baylor." Hope held out her hand, wiggling her hot pink fingernails.

"Fine," I said, reaching for her hand. "But for the record, this won't be good."

Hope looked at Kori. "Let's get her outta here before she changes her mind."

In the hallway, Mr. Byrd pressed his hand to his heart. "Baylor! Don't ever scare me like that again."

"Sorry," I said.

Everyone followed Mr. Byrd through the hallway to a room with Benton Bluff Junior High scrawled on a sheet of paper taped to the door. It had our audition time.

I glanced at the clock. Thirty-two minutes. In thirty-two minutes, our band would play for the judges. And I'd play my solo. I wished that time could fly so this day would be over.

"Instruments ready?" Mr. Byrd asked. "Let's warm up a bit. Someone will be here shortly to let us know it's our turn."

Afterward, Mr. Byrd asked, "Baylor, are you still feeling okay?"

I nodded. "Mostly."

"Remember," Kori said, "deep breathing."

"And relax your muscles, too." Lem pretended to squish a ball in each hand.

"Don't forget to laugh," Zac added. "Picture the judges in their bathing suits."

"Imagine yourself playing perfectly," Hope said, "while the judges sit there wearing little swim caps."

"Yeah, their heads look like turtles." Zac grinned.

I could picture turtle judges, all lined up in a row. And I smiled just a little, too.

"You've all given Baylor some great advice," Mr. Byrd said. "Let's all try some deep breathing."

"Wait, are you nervous, too?" I asked Mr. Byrd. He looked as laid-back as the dolphins on his slightly dressier than normal tropical shirt.

"Sure, everybody gets nervous sometimes, Baylor. In fact, a little bit of stage fright is healthy," he said. "It keeps us on our toes."

After some breathing exercises, Mr. Byrd said, "No matter what happens today, I want you to know how proud I am of you all. It wasn't easy getting here." He looked at Kori and Lem. "Sometimes, it felt like our band might fall apart, didn't it?"

Lem and Kori looked at each other. He smiled. She stuck out her tongue before smiling back.

Then Mr. Byrd looked at me. "But we kept going. Now we're playing stronger than ever as a unit."

He was right about that. When we played "Flight of the Bumblebee" in practice all week, our bees had never sounded more alive.

"Today, if we have a little bobble or two," Mr. Byrd went on, "just keep playing. Don't stop and say, 'Oh, man! I messed up, Byrd!' Just keep fighting through the song. Understood?"

A lady in a gray pantsuit knocked. "Mr. Byrd?"

Mr. Byrd pumped his fist in the air. "Play like the musicians you are!" That was the last thing he said before we shuffled down the hall to audition.

On the way, Kori looked at Lem and said, "We've so got this!" Then they high-fived each other. Just a few days ago, they couldn't stand to be in a room together! But that's the way band kids are. Sometimes we argue, but we also stick together.

Just like the band was there for me. I glanced around. Hope smiled at me. Sherman gave me a thumbs-up. Zac crossed his eyes, and I smiled. Whatever happened, our band was in this together.

Mr. Byrd led us into a huge auditorium. Chairs and music stands stood in a half-circle on the stage, framed on each side by velvety red curtains draped from the ceiling to the floor. Our audience was five judges, sitting in a line a few rows back.

The band filed onstage. Mr. Byrd turned to face us and moved his hands. We knew the cue. We all sat down in unison just like we'd rehearsed.

I stared out at the judges who'd decide if we got to play for the governor. And I was way calmer than I'd thought I'd be.

Until one of the judges said, "Mr. Byrd, is your band ready?" Suddenly, sweat practically dripped from my palms. I wiped them on my dress pants.

Mr. Byrd said, "Yes, sir. We're ready."

That's when my heart stopped beating and did jumping jacks in my chest instead.

They're turtles, just like Zac said, I told myself. I tried picturing them with shells, too. One judge looked grouchy, like a snapping turtle. Seriously.

Mr. Byrd turned back to us. He flashed a reassuring smile. And it was hard to tell with the glare on his glasses, but he might've even winked.

I waited for Mr. Byrd's signal to begin. As soon as he raised his hands up in front of him, everyone in the band brought their instruments to their lips. We'd practiced that over and over. Mr. Byrd had said even the tiniest details of our presentation were important.

"One and two and . . . ," Mr. Byrd counted.

Nothing else mattered then. The judges disappeared. My mind cleared. I focused on the sheet music in front of me. I took a deep breath.

Our bees hummed and then took flight as we played measure after measure. Each line we played brought me closer to the section I dreaded

most—my solo. And then there it was, at the top of the third page.

The rest of the band stopped, while I was supposed to keep playing. But I froze. My fingers hovered above my keys, like a bee hovering above a rose blossom. I felt like I hung in midair, but only for a second.

Mr. Byrd told us we were supposed to keep playing, no matter what. "Fight through the song!" he'd said. And someone playing saxophone did. The sax played the first few notes of my solo, and my fingers thawed. For the rest of the section, our bees buzzed together.

Then the rest of the band joined in. Soon the flight ended. And so did our song.

Mr. Byrd signaled for us to stand before turning to the judges and leading our bow. The snapping turtle judge smiled.

Mr. Byrd headed offstage, and our band followed one row at a time. We'd practiced our exit, too. Mr. Byrd said we'd look polished, and he was right.

And since I had just mega-flubbed my solo, we needed all the polish we could get.

"I'm sorry! It's all my fault! I let everybody down! I knew I was the wrong choice for the solo!" I fought back tears when I stopped to breathe.

Hope put her arm around me. "It's okay, Baylor."

"Yeah," Kori said. "It wasn't that bad."

"Really?" I looked up then.

"*Oui*, you did great," Lem said.

"You and Zac," Sherman added.

"Zac?" I asked. *What did Zac have to do with it?*

Mr. Byrd nodded. "Zac played your solo with you. Although, with you two playing together, it wasn't a solo." He laughed. "It was a duet."

"Zac?" I couldn't believe it. "But—"

"No way! Baylor is speechless!" Zac joked.

"But I thought you never practiced," I said.

"I didn't. Until you said to play outside," Zac said. "Remember at the party I said I had a surprise?"

"Yeah," I said.

Zac grinned. "That's why I was late. I was giving the rabbits and squirrels a free concert."

"But I was too upset to listen," I said. "I'm sorry." I'd apologized before, but now I felt bad all over again.

"No big deal," Zac said.

"It is a big deal. You were awesome, Zac," I said.

"Nah." His cheeks turned pink. "Okay, a little."

Everybody laughed then. Until there was a knock on the door. The lady in the pantsuit was back. It was time to find out if we'd won. Or not.

Chapter 12
FLYING HIGH

When we had auditioned earlier, the auditorium was empty except for the judges. Now it was packed with fifteen junior high bands, all excited to find out which two had won. It sounded like a party in there until the snapping turtle judge walked onstage holding a microphone.

"Welcome, everyone! I'm Nathaniel Tatman. On behalf of these other fine judges and myself, I'd like to thank you for attending today's competition. Excellent work." Tatman Turtle clapped. "Give yourselves a hand!"

The room erupted in clapping. When everyone settled down again, he continued, "Are you ready to find out which two bands were selected to play at the governor's mansion centennial celebration?"

I wasn't sure if I was ready or not. I mean, the band wasn't mad that I froze during the audition. But if we lost, I'd always blame myself.

Tatman Turtle smiled when one of the other judges handed him a slip of paper. "Here we go! First, we have the Albert Y. Ross Junior High band, directed by Mrs. Emily King!"

Applause and cheers thundered across the room. And it wasn't hard to figure out which band that was. They were the kids near the front, jumping out of their seats and screaming.

When their band director finally got them back into their seats, Tatman Turtle continued. "We have one spot left." Then he practically shouted into the microphone. "And it belongs to the Benton Bluff Junior High band, directed by Mr. Elliot Byrd!"

"Us? Did he say us?" I asked.

But nobody heard me because the kids in our band were jumping out of their seats, shouting and celebrating. I jumped out of my seat, too. Hope and

I hopped up and down, just like the contestants who win big prizes on the game shows my Nana watches on TV.

Our celebration didn't last long. "Everyone, please sit," Mr. Byrd said. He held up a finger to shush us, but there was a huge smile behind it.

After that, Tatman Turtle went on about how it was a hard choice and how he wished they had room for all the bands. Then he thanked everyone again and dismissed us. Bands began filing out to find their buses in the parking lot. But our band couldn't leave until we picked up information about the celebration at the governor's mansion.

When the auditorium cleared out, Tatman Turtle came walking toward us. "Mr. Byrd, congratulations!" He held out his hand.

Mr. Byrd shook it. "Thank you, sir."

"And congratulations to you all!" Tatman Turtle added. "Let me say, not only are you a very talented group of kids, the judges and I were impressed by your composure and the way you presented yourselves onstage." He winked then. "The governor is in for a treat!"

So Tatman Turtle wasn't a snapping turtle after all. He was a very nice turtle. And fast, too. He marched away to congratulate the other winners.

"Can you believe we won, Mr. Byrd?" Sherman asked.

"Sherman," Mr. Byrd said, "I felt like we'd already won before we ever stepped foot on that stage."

"Band directors get paid to say stuff like that," Zac joked.

Mr. Byrd smiled. "I really mean it, though. I believed in your talent. And I believed in you."

"Even me?" Zac asked.

"Even you, Zac." Mr. Byrd laughed.

"Hey!" Zac said. "Let's have a party to celebrate."

"Will you bring more balloons?" I asked.

Zac laughed. "How'd you know it was me?"

"They don't call me Fuzzy Waffles for nothing, you know." I smiled. "Thanks for bringing them." And I still hadn't forgotten what Zac did for me at the audition. "Thanks for saving my solo, too, Zac."

"You're welcome." He smiled. "Just remember you owe me one."

"Have your agent call my agent," I joked back.

On the way to our bus, Lem said, "See, Kori? I told you we had this." He held up his trumpet case. "All thanks to *moi*."

I held my breath. But Kori didn't let Lem have it. She just patted her trombone case and smiled. "You mean all thanks to Russell. And to *moi*."

"Hey!" Zac said, pointing to himself. "Don't you mean *moi*?"

Everyone laughed and started getting in on it, too. Even Mr. Byrd said, "No, it was *moi*!"

"Stop already," I said, laughing too. "It was you, and you, and you." I pointed to all of them. "It was all of you."

"Baylor's right." Zac grinned. "Obviously we're all awesome!"

Everyone started celebrating all over again.

I knew Zac was joking. But he was right. This band, our band, really was awesome.

"We're kind of like the bees in 'Flight of the Bumblebee.' When bees work together, they make sweet honey," I said. "And we sounded pretty sweet today."

"Yeah, and sometimes we sting, just like real bees," Zac said.

Kori and Lem pretended to sting each other.

I smiled. "But we still fit together, like one giant honeycomb."

"That's just sappy, Baylor," Zac teased.

"I know." I smiled. It really was sappy. But I was proud of our awesome band.

And when we played at the governor's mansion next month, he'd get to see how awesome we were, too. I couldn't wait!